Mom, Dad, Come Back Soon

Published by
MAGINATION PRESS
An Educational Publishing Foundation Book
American Psychological Association
750 First Street, NE
Washington, DC 20002

For more information about our books, including a complete catalog, please write to us,
call 1-800-374-2721, or visit our website at www.maginationpress.com.

Editor: Darcie Conner Johnston
Art Director: Susan K. White
The text type is Basilia

Library of Congress Cataloging-in-Publication Data

Pappas, Debra.
Mom, Dad, come back soon / by Debra Pappas ; illustrated by Carol Koeller.
p.   cm.
Summary: While his parents are away for a few days Tyler has fun staying with
his best friend Cindy's family, even though he sometimes feels lonely or afraid.
Includes a note to parents about helping a child cope with their absence.
ISBN 1-55798-799-8 (hc. : alk. paper)—ISBN 1-55798-798-X (pbk. : alk. paper).
[1. Separation anxiety—Fiction. 2. Parent and child—Fiction. 3. Best friends—Fiction.
4. Friendship—Fiction.] I. Koeller, Carol, ill. II. Title.

PZ7.P21175 Mo 2001
[E]—dc21   2001030892

Manufactured in the United States of America
10 9 8 7 6 5 4 3 2 1

Mom, Dad, Come Back Soon

written by
Debra Pappas, Ph.D.

illustrated by
Carol Koeller

MAGINATION PRESS • WASHINGTON, DC

For Matt and Theo, my two bright stars – DP

To my family and family friends – CK

Tyler was helping Mom pack his suitcase. He picked up Monkey, his favorite stuffed animal. "You're coming too, Monkey," he said.

"Do you want to bring anything else?" Mom asked.

Tyler looked around his room. He was going to spend a few days at his friend Cindy's house while his parents went on a trip. Maybe he should bring his toy dinosaur. Cindy liked dinosaurs as much as he did. He took it off the shelf and handed it to Mom.

Mom showed Tyler a picture taken last summer. It was of Mom, Dad, and Tyler at the beach. They were making a gigantic sandcastle. Tyler smiled. He remembered how they laughed when a big wave came along and almost knocked it over.

"I will put this picture in your suitcase, too," said Mom.
"You can look at it when you're thinking of us."

Why can't I go with you this time?" Tyler asked.

"Sometimes Mom and Dad need time alone together," said Mom,
giving him a big hug. "We'll miss you, and you'll miss us too.
But you'll have lots of fun with Cindy, and Dad and I will have
a nice time, and soon we'll all be back home together."

Tyler had asked Mom and Dad this question before.
He asked again, because he liked to hear the answer.

Downstairs, Dad took the calendar off the wall. "Look," he said, pointing to a square with a smiley face. "This is today, the day that we leave." Dad moved his finger down a row of squares and pointed to a bright gold star. "And right here, this is the day when we come home."

Tyler looked at the square with the smiley face and the square with the gold star. He noticed that other squares had little drawings in them, too. He saw an elephant, a birthday cake, and a telephone. "What happens on those days?" he asked.

"Lots of fun things," said Dad. "You are going to the zoo with Cindy's family. Your cousin Tommy is having a birthday party. And the telephone means that Mom and I will call you from our hotel."

"You can cross off each day if you want," said Dad. "Then you can tell how many days are left until we come home."

Tyler was happy that he was going to Cindy's house. But he was also a little bit nervous. In the car, his stomach felt a little strange. He told Mom, and she said it might be butterflies. "Not real butterflies, of course," she said. "That's just a way of saying that you feel excited."

Cindy was Tyler's best friend. He had played at her house many times. He had even spent the night there, but the next morning he had come home. This was different.

At the red light, Mom looked at Tyler. "Maybe you feel a little scared, too," she said gently. "That's okay. I think you'll be surprised by how much fun you'll have. And we'll be home before you know it."

Cindy and her mother were sitting
on the front steps. Cindy jumped up when she saw Tyler
and his mom and dad get out of the car. "Let's go make a fort!"
she said, pulling Tyler toward the backyard. Tyler was excited.
He and Cindy loved to make forts. Mom and Dad gave Tyler big
hugs, and everyone waved as they drove away.

All afternoon, Tyler and Cindy played together. They had lots of fun. Sometimes they played with Cindy's little brother, Robby. They played pirates in the sandbox and going-camping under a big tree. During a race, Tyler fell down and scraped his knee. He wished his mom was there to kiss it. Cindy said, "My mom can help."

Cindy's mother washed the scrape and told Tyler he could pick out his favorite bandage. He chose one with a bright green dinosaur. Then she put an extra dinosaur bandage on his shirt. "That's for being brave," she said, and gave Tyler a hug. "All better now?" she asked. Tyler smiled. Yes, his knee didn't hurt at all anymore.

When it was time for dinner,
Tyler was very hungry. Cindy's father
served him some meatloaf and mashed
potatoes.

Tyler did not like mashed potatoes.
He loved meatloaf, but this meatloaf did
not taste at all like the meatloaf at his
own house.

Cindy passed Tyler a basket of warm
rolls. They smelled really good. "I do like
these," thought Tyler, and he took two.

14

He put lots of butter and honey on them.
At home, they only had rolls on special occasions,
like holidays and birthdays. "Can I have one
more?" he asked when the second one was gone.

"You sure can," said Cindy's mother, smiling.
"I'm glad you like them!"

Dinner at Cindy's house was much noisier than it
was at home. Cindy's father told some funny jokes.
Robby banged his spoon on the highchair tray and
sang a song. Cindy started a guessing game.
Tyler thought dinner at Cindy's was fun.

"Time for baths!" said Cindy's mother.

Robby got the first bath and Cindy got the second. When it was Tyler's turn, the bathroom floor was wet and the soap was soggy. The only bath toy was a little blue sailboat.

Tyler wished he had brought Super Frog with him. Baths were more fun when he could wind up Super Frog and make him swim. He put the sailboat in the water. He made little waves with his hand and watched the sailboat go up and down. "Ahoy, mates," he said. "A storm is coming!"

Then he made a really big wave, and the sailboat spun around and around. Tyler laughed. He thought he would like to have a little blue sailboat of his own at home. He played so long the water turned cold.

Just before bed, Cindy's mother made a special treat. She gave them each a mug of warm cocoa with marshmallows. Tyler thought it tasted wonderful. Then she said, "Tyler gets to pick the story tonight!"

Cindy and Robby had lots of books. They were different from Tyler's books at home. He picked out a book about a big friendly moose who liked strawberry ice cream cones. Cindy's mother read the story. She made a great moose's voice, with a low, rumbly laugh. Tyler was happy he had picked that book. Cindy and Robby liked it, too.

Tyler took Monkey and snuggled into his sleeping bag on Cindy's floor. He felt warm and cozy. But when Cindy's mother turned out the lights, he saw a scary shadow on the wall.

Tyler hugged Monkey as hard as he could. He wished he was home in his own room. He wished Mom and Dad were there.

The more he
thought about home,
the sadder he felt. And the
sadder he felt, the madder he got
that his Mom and Dad went away and left
him with scary shadows. "I want to go home,"
he called out loud. "I want my Mom and Dad."

19

Cindy's father heard Tyler. He stuck his head in the door and asked, "Is there anything wrong?" Tyler told him about the scary shadow. Cindy's father turned on the hall light, but Cindy said it was too bright.

"I know what we can do," said Cindy's father. He left and came back with a little nightlight. It plugged right into the wall and gave the room a soft yellow glow. The light did not bother Cindy, and it made the scary shadow go away. "There, that shadow is gone now," said Cindy's father. Tyler felt much better. "The shadow is gone," he said to himself. Soon he was sound asleep.

After breakfast, Tyler crossed off another square on his calendar. For a few minutes, he looked at the picture Mom had given him. He showed it to Cindy and told her all about the beach and the sandcastle. Then they went outside to make castles in the sandbox with Robby. When Robby knocked the castles down, they pretended he was a giant wave.

Dinner that evening was spaghetti, Tyler's favorite. He ate a second helping. Robby picked out the bedtime story. It was a funny one about a dog from outer space. Afterward, Tyler went right to sleep.

When Dad and Mom called from their
hotel the next day, Tyler was right in
the middle of playing Go Fish with Cindy.
He jumped up and ran to the phone.

Tyler told Mom and Dad
about all the fun he was
having at Cindy's house. He
listened as they told him
about their trip. Mom
said, "I love you
bunches," just like
at home. She blew
Tyler a kiss over
the phone and
asked, "Did you get
it?" Tyler said yes,
and blew one back.

After they hung up, Tyler went back to the card game, but he didn't feel like playing anymore. He didn't want a snack, either. He just wanted Mom and Dad to come home. Cindy's mother gave him a hug. "They'll be home soon," she said gently.

Tyler got out his calendar and counted all the
squares that he had not crossed off. Cindy's
mother was right! Mom and Dad would be home
soon. He wondered if they missed him as much
as he missed them. He hoped they did.

The next day, Cindy's mother and father took everyone to the zoo. They ate ice cream and saw lots of animals. When they got back, Tyler drew a picture of the zoo for Mom and Dad. He put some hearts around the edges.

Tyler was outside playing with Cindy when Mom and Dad pulled up in their car. He ran to them as fast as he could. Mom and Dad hugged and kissed Tyler. He gave them the picture of the zoo that he had drawn. They said they were proud of him, and Tyler felt proud of himself, too. "I really liked staying at Cindy's house," he said, "but I am glad you're home."

27

Dad put Tyler's suitcase in the car. Tyler said goodbye to Cindy and her family. Cindy's mother hugged him. "We loved having you stay with us," she said.

"Hurry back so we can work some more on our fort," said Cindy. "You can sleep over again, or maybe I can sleep over at your house!"

"Okay!" Tyler promised as he climbed in the backseat with Monkey.

On the way home, Tyler asked, "Are you going to go away again?"

"Not for a long time," said Dad.

"Can we go to the beach again this summer?"

"Absolutely," said Mom.

"And build another sandcastle?"

"Maybe three sandcastles," said Dad, smiling. "We'll have lots of fun together!"

Tyler smiled and hugged Monkey. "Good," he said.

Note to Parents

BY JANE ANNUNZIATA, PSY.D.

From time to time as children are growing up, their parents are temporarily absent for business trips, weekends away for themselves, or longer vacations of a week or so. These separations are an inevitable part of family life and, in truth, are beneficial for both children and parents if planned and handled with care. Parents can help their children accept and successfully manage an absence in two ways: by understanding what children experience when parents are away from home, and by using an array of practical coping techniques before, during, and after a separation.

Arrangements for Care

"Who will take care of me?" This is often the first question children ask when they learn that their parents will be traveling. They want to feel safe and comfortable, and they tend to focus on such questions as "Will I like the food?" and "Can I ride my bike there?" Parents want most to know that their children will be safe and well cared for; otherwise, they will have difficulty relaxing and enjoying themselves.

- **THE CAREGIVER.** Carefully picking the caregiver is the single most important thing you can do to ensure a successful time away. Choose someone whom both you and your children like a lot, know well, and feel comfortable with. When possible, give your child or children some control in choosing the caregiver.
- **LOCATION.** Children generally prefer having the caregiver come to their own home rather than having to stay in a less familiar environment. This can increase their feelings of comfort, but it is not essential and, when possible, can be a "choice point," thus giving your kids some say. Choices always help them feel better!
- **SIBLINGS.** When children have siblings, and when it is possible, having brothers and sisters stay together with the same caregiver can provide support and company. This is especially helpful for younger children and during longer stays.
- **BUILDING UP TO OVERNIGHT CARE.** Before attempting the first overnight separation, your child should be entirely comfortable with the caregiver for an extended period, such as a full day. Children need small, short "practices" apart from parents before longer and farther separations are attempted. Thus, it's best to have your first trip be within an hour from home and only for one night. Try this several times with good success before increasing the stakes. The length of time a child can manage depends on several

factors, including the relationship with the caregiver, age and maturity level of the child, and the child's feelings and reactions to separations. You may want to consult your pediatrician before scheduling a longer vacation.

Feelings About Being Left Behind

Children don't like to be left behind. This feeling is almost universal, but is especially true of younger kids and only children. They want to be included. They don't understand why their parents want or need to go away without them. They worry that their parents don't want to be with them. They don't like missing out on something good. Your child may have any and all of these thoughts and feelings.

- **EXPLAIN ABOUT GROWN-UP TIME.** Explain to your child why parents go away on their own. For example, you might say, "Mom and Dad love our time with you, and we really have fun when we do things all together. But adults need grown-up time to be all by ourselves, too, just like kids need time alone with their friends. You know how you feel when your friends come over to play? You like to play just with them, even though at other times you enjoy doing things with your parents. That's kind of how adults feel." Of course, the tone of this should be adjusted for the age and maturity level of the child.
- **EXPLAIN ABOUT FAMILY TIME.** At the same time, validate how much you value your time with your children. This helps to ease the sting. You might end a statement like the one above by referring to something the family will do together, such as, "Mom and Dad are looking forward to our weekend alone together, but we're also really looking forward to our family vacation at the beach."

Worries About Being Forgotten

When parents are away, children worry that they will be forgotten or that their parents won't be thinking about them. This can contribute to the anxiety children often feel during such separations.

- **VERBALIZE YOUR "MISSING" FEELINGS.** Before you go, tell your children (as often as they need to hear it) that you will think and talk about them a lot while you are away. At the same time, let them know that you will be fine without them and they will do fine without you. Otherwise, children may think they are supposed to be unhappy while Mom and Dad are away to show how much they love and miss them. It also helps to say that parents and children can feel close to each other even when they aren't together.

- **CALENDAR.** Give children a calendar so that they can follow your vacation and feel connected to you. It will also help them keep track of how long you'll be gone. Kids feel a sense of psychological control as they mark out or put stickers on the days. Also, try to involve the child in the making or choosing of the calendar or its stickers. This sense of control helps to decrease some of the negative reactions children can have when their parents are away.

- **PRE-CALENDAR.** For very young children who do not know their numbers or know how to count, use concrete objects to mark the time that you will be away. A small, simple clothesline and clothespins work very well. String the clothesline with pins to represent the number of days that you will be gone, and at the end of each day your young child can have the satisfaction (and sense of control) of removing a pin. Explain this system before you leave, and have your caregiver do the same during your time away.

- **PACK AN OBJECT OF YOUR CHILD'S.** Ask your children for an object of theirs that you can pack and take with you. You might say, "Mom and Dad would like to take something of yours with us [e.g., a toy car, a small stuffed animal]. We're going to put it in our hotel room, and every time we look at it we'll think of you. Of course, we'll think of you anyway, but every time we look at that red car sitting on our dresser, we'll smile remembering how much fun you have playing with your cars." You may also take a framed picture of your children, and let them know that you are doing this, but children, especially the younger ones, seem to really like the idea of giving their parents a toy of theirs to tuck in their suitcase.

- **LEAVE SOMETHING OF YOURS.** A picture of both parents is very useful. Also, give your child something to carry around. This can be anything, such as a comb, a notepad, a case of business cards, and so on. Even babies and toddlers can be given something of their parents' to ease the stress they feel. A t-shirt that smells like Mom or Dad can go in a baby's crib, or be carried around or even worn, providing the child with comfort and feelings of security.

- **MAIL.** Children love mail. Send your children a postcard or note as you are leaving town, so that they receive it within a day or two, and continue to send cards daily while away. You can also leave short, simple notes with their caregiver.

For example, you might say, "I hope you're having a good weekend. We'll be thinking of you and your soccer game and zoo trip this Saturday. Hope you have fun!" Referencing their activities helps keep the connection strong. And finally, e-mail and faxes provide instant letters that parents and children can send to each other as a way to stay in touch.

- **PHONE HOME.** Brief daily phone calls go a long way in helping kids (and parents) feel in touch. A detailed message on an answering machine is a good second choice. When talking or leaving a message, be positive about how and what you are doing, but don't be overly glowing. That will only lead to increased feelings of resentment. Also, make reference to something that the child has done or will be doing while you are apart. You might say, "We are fine. We had a relaxing day. I hope you had fun at your gymnastics class. We'll call again tomorrow."

  A note about phone calls: Don't be surprised or alarmed if your child refuses to talk with you. Most children are happy when their parents call, but it is not uncommon for them to express anger or upset by refusing to engage on the phone. First, talk with your caregiver (maybe the child just woke up from a nap, or there has just been a sibling squabble, or today's music lesson was difficult, etc.). If the child will at least come to the phone and hold it, you can say you wonder if his lack of talking is a way of showing feelings and suggest that he will feel better if he can talk to you about it. If that doesn't work, suggest that he talk about what is bothering him with the caregiver, and then bring the incident up when you are back at home, so that he can learn better ways to cope with his feelings.

- **RETURN-HOME ACTIVITY.** Before you leave for your trip, make a plan about something that you and your child will do together upon your return. You might say, "When Mom and Dad come home, let's try out this new brownie mix. I'll leave it right here on the counter to remind you that we'll be doing this when we come back on Sunday." In the child's young mind, this offers a great deal of reassurance as well as something tangible to hold on to.

Feelings of Anger

Children generally feel angry when their parents go off on their own. The most common scenario is that they behave well for their caregivers and often seem (and really are) happy while their parents are away. But once the parents return home, the floodgates of anger open in one form or another!

The child usually starts misbehaving, acting rude, or expressing anger in response to reasonable, everyday requests that parents make. Although it is frustrating (especially for parents) when children can't simply voice their anger constructively and directly, it is not surprising that most children have trouble doing so—or that they may even be unaware they are feeling angry at all. Anger can be a disconcerting emotion to experience. Children love their moms and dads so much! It is upsetting to feel angry toward anyone so beloved.

For the parents' part, they often find themselves feeling annoyed and disappointed. They may have tried to do everything "right" during their time away, but they still end up feeling rejected. And the child's difficult behavior brings to a sudden end the oasis of relaxation they had while they were away. It helps to give yourself permission to feel disappointment and annoyance while putting your energy into working with your child's anger so that things settle down as quickly as possible.

- **BE PREPARED!** Anticipate that your child will express angry verbal and non-verbal responses to your absence. It is often hard for parents to believe and accept that feelings of anger will occur when they go away. But this is a nearly universal reaction.
- **BEFORE YOU GO.** The most effective way to help children cope with their anger is simply to talk with them about these feelings before your trip. For example, you could say to your child, "Sometimes kids feel angry when their parents go away together. This is a common thing, and nothing to worry about. Anger is just like any other feeling. If you feel angry, you can talk about it, or you can draw a picture of your feelings, or go outside and kick a ball. This usually helps a lot. It also helps to remember that while we're away, you'll be having fun with your grandparents and doing neat things, too."
- **AFTER YOU RETURN.** Upon your return, the best way to handle feelings of anger is to move in quickly. If you suspect that anger is behind an unhappy attitude or uncooperative behavior (and it often is), you might say, "I've noticed that you've been acting grumpy since Dad and I returned from our trip. I wonder if you're a little annoyed with us for going away? Let's talk about it and see if it helps." Or you could say, "You never used to give us a hard time when we said it's time for bed, but now it seems you're trying to turn bedtime into a fight. Maybe this really isn't about going to bed. Maybe you're angry with us for taking a weekend away without you. Let's talk about that and see if it makes bedtime easier."

- **DON'T MINIMIZE.** Parents often want to minimize the anger that children experience because the anger makes them feel uncomfortable about being away. Remind yourself that a child's getting angry is not a good reason to stay home! It is beneficial for children to have the opportunity to get angry with their parents, to practice expressing this emotion constructively, and to be able to work it through.
- **RESOLVING FEELINGS THROUGH TALK.** Parents may worry that addressing the possibility of angry feelings either before they depart or after they return will increase these feelings or suggest feelings that weren't there to begin with. But the opposite is actually true. Just talking about anger helps kids feel better, manage their anger better, and feel less bothered by this normal emotion. Paradoxically, talking about anger helps children feel less angry.

Benefits of Time Apart

Parents tend to worry about leaving their children overnight, even for just a night or two. While children can have many reactions to even short absences, it is also very important to remember that there are many benefits for both parents and kids when this occurs.

When parents go away for time to themselves, they are doing something good for their children, too. Nothing benefits children more than having parents whose relationship is happy and stable, and who have ample emotional and physical energy for the daunting task of parenting. Time away from your children not only nourishes your relationship but also helps each parent separately to feel well nurtured. In short, when parents are able to recharge their batteries (and going away even for one night is a great recharger), they are optimally able to be "on" for their kids.

Finally, when you go away, your children have an opportunity to practice and eventually master the difficult feelings that arise for all of us with separations. (This is true as well when they go away to camp, spend the night at friends' houses, and so on.) Life is filled with separations, large and small good-byes, and leave takings. Children need to know that they can handle the myriad of feelings that inevitably occur in these situations. When well-managed, time apart from your children can be a win-win situation for all. Happy travels!

JANE ANNUNZIATA, PSY.D., is a clinical psychologist with a private practice for children and families in McLean, Virginia. She is also the author of several books and articles addressing the concerns of children and parents.

JP, t

Pappas, Debra.

Mom, Dad, come back
soon.

$14.95

DATE			